The New Kid

Marie-Louise Fitzpatrick

Hodder
Children's
Books

A division of Hachette Children's Books

There's a new kid on our street.
Our mums say we have to ask
her out to play.

Her mum says she
has to wear her coat.
We're not wearing coats.

"What's your name?" someone asks.
"Ellie," says the new kid.

"Ellie-in-the-grey-coat," someone says.

"Ellie-in-the-grey-coat," we all chant.

"Ellie-elephant," Jodie squeals.
"ELLIE-ELEPHANT!" we all shout.
We fall about laughing.

The new kid
says nothing.

She hides her head inside her grey coat.

"Weirdo," someone says.

"We-ir-do," my friends chant.

I say nothing.

"What's she doing?" someone asks.

The new kid is being an elephant.

She waves her grey trunk in the air.

"Ellie-elephant," we shout, and laugh again.

The elephant charges.

Oh, oh!

We all scream and run away.

But we come back.

"Now what's she doing?" someone says.
She's being a seal. She claps her flippers.
Everyone claps too.

Everyone except me.

I make up the games our gang play. What if this new kid makes up better games than me?

The new kid pulls her arms out of her coat sleeves and runs up and down the street. She's being a superhero.

That does it!

I go quick, quick to my house and grab my coat.
I run after the new kid.

We're two superheroes.

Now everyone has a coat.

"SUPERHEROES!" we all yell.

We fly up and down the street till we
are so hot we all fall down in a heap.
We throw off our coats.
Except the new kid. She keeps hers on.

She smiles at me.
I smile back.

There's a new kid on our street.

Her name is **Ellie.** And she's my **friend.**